Brides Are No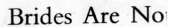

CIJ00722019

Rupa Creative Writing

New Poetry

Tabish Khair
My World
A Reporter's Diary

Anna Sujatha Mathai
The Attic of Night

Makarand Paranjape
The Serene Flame
Playing the Dark God
*An Anthology of New Indian
English Poetry*

Tara Patel
Single Woman

Sudeep Sen
The Lunar Visitations

Ranjit Hoskote
Zones of Assault

Sitakant Mahapatra
Death of Krishna & Other Poems

Hoshang Merchant
Flower to Flame

Rachna Joshi
Configurations

Bibhu Padhi
A Wound Elsewhere

Prabhanjan K Mishra
Vigil

Sanjiv Bhatla
Haiku, My Friend

Ashok Mahajan
Uniformly Crazy

New Fiction

Anurag Mathur
The Inscrutable Americans

Aniruddha Bahal
A Crack in the Mirror

Dina Mehta
And Some Take a Lover

New Stories

M T Vasudevan Nair
*Catching an Elephant and
Other Stories*

Dina Mehta
*Miss Menon Did Not Believe
in Magic*

New Drama

Mohan Rakesh
Adhe Adhure

Brides Are
Not for Burning

A Play in Two Acts

Dina Mehta

Rupa & Co

CALCUTTA

ALLAHABAD BOMBAY DELHI

© Dina Mehta 1993

An Original Rupa Paperback

First published 1993 by
Rupa & Co

7/16 Ansari Road, Daryaganj, New Delhi 110 002
15 Bankim Chatterjee Street, Calcutta 700 073
135 South Malaka, Allahabad 211 001
P. G. Solanki Path, Lamington Road, Bombay 400 007

Typeset in 12/13 Bembo by
Megatechnics
19A Ansari Road
New Delhi 110 002

Printed in India by
Gopsons Papers Pvt Ltd
A-28 Sector IX
Noida 201 301

Rs 50

ISBN 81-7167-114-4

*All applications for permission to stage this play
in English or in any other language, whether by amateurs
or professionals, must be made in writing to
Ms Dina Mehta, 2A Anita, Mount Pleasant Road,
Malabar Hill, Bombay 400 006, India.
No performance may take place unless
permission has first been obtained.*

To

All the angry young women
Who can be whatever they choose to be

Acknowledgements

Brides Are Not for Burning won the first prize in a worldwide playwriting competition sponsored by the BBC in 1979. It was broadcast from London on their World Service and later by All India Radio. Its stage version, published here, has been performed in Madras, Bangalore and Bombay.

Characters
in order of appearance

FATHER: At 70, the oldest member of the Desai family. He is twice-married.

MALINI: His 20-year-old daughter. A college student, unmarried, and sister of the young housewife who has died of burns.

ANIL: A 22-year-old schoolteacher, brother of Malini and the dead woman. Unmarried.

ROY: A young anarchist, a professional lover of mankind. About 27 years old, married.

PROFESSOR PALKAR: Professor of History at the university, over 55 years of age. Anil is his former student.

SANJAY: Malini's boyfriend, Anil's college friend. About 23 years old.

VINOD: Husband of the dead woman, Laxmi, brother-in-law of Malini and Anil. About 28 years old.

TARLA: Friend and neighbour of the dead woman, Laxmi. About 25 years old.

MOTHER-IN-LAW: Mother of Vinod and Arjun, mother-in-law of Laxmi, the dead woman. About 51 years old.

KALU: Elderly servant employed by Vinod's family. He is about 58.

ARJUN: Vinod's younger brother, a fat boy in his late teens.

Setting

Altogether five separate acting areas are needed, designed sparingly and with a degree of flexibility, and independent of each other as far as the lighting is concerned. Act One requires only one change of scene, Act Two requires four. Both the Acts have the major acting area in common, where four of the total of eight scenes are enacted.

The acting areas are as follows:

1. The DESAI tenement room is the major and the most detailed area. It is shabbily furnished with a chair with hand-rests for FATHER, a string bed, a rickety table loaded with books with a straight chair drawn into it, and a large trunk covered with an old sari under a corner window with bars. The walls display a clothes peg, a washline and a couple of garish calendars portraying Hindu gods and goddesses. The room is accessible by a front door and another door leads into the kitchen.

2. SANJAY's living-room requires a well-upholstered sofa with a chair which belongs with it, and a luxurious-looking rug on the floor.

3. VINOD's office is only a table with files and papers strewn on it, two chairs and a telephone.

4. TARLA's kitchen requires a parapet (or stand) with a kerosene stove and a few utensils resting on it, and a stool.

5. The IN-LAWS' living-cum-dining room section requires a bare dining table with chairs, a stool for KALU to sit on, paring vegetables, and a TV set (or wall unit or show-case) in the foreground to suggest the living room area. One open doorway left leads to the inner rooms, including the kitchen; the front door is right off-stage.

Note: Areas 2, 3, 4 and 5 can be as small as possible, and perhaps interchangeable, in which case fewer confining areas need be mapped out on the stage.

The break-up of the scenes is as follows:

Act One:
Scene 1:   The Desai tenement room
Scene 2:   The Desai tenement room
Scene 3:   Sanjay's living-room

Act Two:
Scene 1:   The Desai tenement room
Scene 2:   Vinod's office
Scene 3:   Tarla's kitchen
Scene 4:   The in-laws' living-cum-dining room
Scene 5:   The Desai tenement room

Act One

Scene 1

The Desai tenement room, poorly lit. It is about 7 p.m. and MALINI, *who is awaiting her brother, is pacing the floor restlessly.* FATHER *has fallen asleep in his chair, open newspaper on his knees. Light goes up on him, showing him to be an old man of 70 odd, head slumped forward on his chest, fragile hands in frayed shirt-cuffs resting on the arms of his chair. As Malini stops abruptly to watch him, he wakes with a start and fumbles for the slipping newspaper with unsteady hands.*

Father: It's not in here, I was telling you. There is no report of it in the papers.
Malini: [*bitterly*] Of course there is no report of it in the papers. We are not important enough.
Father: No report of what?
Malini: What were you looking for?
Father: I don't remember. Where are my spectacles?
Malini: On your nose, Father.
Father: [*touching them*] Oh. The sugar prices have come down, Malini. I read it here somewhere. [*picks up the paper with trembling hands*] Also onions.
Malini: Good.
Father: Did you go to the bazaar today?
Malini: No.
Father: You better send Anil down while there

11

is still a little light. After dusk they sell you poor stuff you can't see. [*looking at the empty bed*] Anil hasn't come home?

Malini: No.

Father: They work him very hard at the school. Well, it's a new job and you must prove yourself at a new job. . .[*breaks off, in thought*] He teaches mathematics?

Malini: History, Father.

Father: I thought maths was his subject. He was very good at maths as a boy. So was I. . . Your mother always got me to total up her purchases. [*looking round vaguely*] She is in the kitchen?

Malini: [*sharply*] Dad! You're allowing your mind to wander again. Of course Mother is not in the kitchen.

Father: Then who's in the kitchen? Laxmi? No no. Laxmi got married five years ago. . . . She never comes to see us these days. It's not like Laxmi . . . not to come and visit me. Has Vinod taken her to Kashmir again?

Malini: No! [*as he tries to struggle to his feet*] Where are you going?

Father: To the kitchen.

Malini: You want a drink of water? Sit! I'll fetch it for you.

Father: I don't want water. I want. . .

Malini: Yes?

Father: [*subsiding in his chair*] I don't remember what I wanted . . . in the kitchen. You said Laxmi is not there?

Malini: No, Father.

Father: No no, of course not. She is . . .[*suddenly

gripping the arms of his chair in terror] Where have they taken her? Where? It was in the papers. Just a small para. . . [*crumples the pages in his agitation*] Where did I read it. . . [*like a child*] Will you find it for me, Malu? On one of the inside pages. . .

Malini: [*snatching the paper furiously away from him*] There is nothing in today's paper, Father.

Father: Nothing? I must have read it yesterday, then. Last week. . . [*sits rigid for a moment, then*] That time when Vinod's uncle flung the 100-rupee notes at my feet because they wanted all those extra guests to be fed at the wedding . . . that was the time to have called off the whole thing. But I swallowed even that insult.

Malini: [*uncompromising*] Yes. Why did you?

Father: [*mumbling*] Marriage is 12 tolas of gold, 2000 rupees for a hall, utensils of steel, saris of silk. . . Their expectations were endless because they imagined a government clerk makes so much on the side. They thought I had feathered my nest with bribes and kickbacks. . . And I let them think that because I wanted to do my best by Laxmi!

Malini: Why did you call her Laxmi? Was it your native optimism? Or a grotesque sense of humour?

Father: What? What? [*with unexpected spirit*] You don't know it is auspicious to call your first child Laxmi? Calling on the goddess of wealth brings prosperity in its wake — you don't know? [*has a brief, violent bout of coughing, then*] It worries me, though, that she has no children. After five years! You were all born in the first five years of marriage. . .

Malini: A pity you had not heard of contraceptives, Father!

Father: [*unheeding*] Laxmi, Anil, you, the twins who lived only a few months. . . Her hips were wide, some women are made for child-bearing . . . unlike poor Sujata, whom I sent back to her parents after ten years. Docile and obedient she was. Sujata. But she miscarried each time she became pregnant. . . I sent her away after ten years and six miscarriages. . . [*mumbling now*] slip of a thing . . . but your mother was curved like a goddess. . . [*paper slips from his hands as he closes his eyes and falls asleep, a pleased smile on his lips which infuriates Malini. As she stoops to pick up the paper,* ANIL *enters by the front door, a load of exercise books in one hand.*]

Malini: [*straightening up*] Anil! I thought you'd never get home. What was the verdict?

Anil: [*placing books on the table, sitting down slowly on the bed*] I'm tired as hell, Malini.

Malini: I'll make you some tea. What was the coroner's ruling?

Anil: What we expected.

Malini: Murder?

Anil: For God's sake, what are you saying? Don't let Father hear you.

Malini: He's fallen asleep in his chair again. Dreaming of women with hips like watermelons.

Anil: [*sharply*] You know I don't like you picking on him.

14

Malini: He never knows when I do it, so why does it worry you?

Anil: [*wearily*] I don't want to start the argument again. I know the old feel your disrespect even when they —

Malini: Live in a fog? Well I think you have to be a saint not to resent sickness or senility in those you have to care for. And I am no saint.

Anil: *That* I can vouch for.

Malini: Good. I'm waiting to hear the verdict.

Anil: Accident.

Malini: [*grimly*] I see. They decided Laxmi's sari was soaked in kerosene by *accident*. A match was set to it by *accident*.

Anil: What's the matter with you? Her sari caught fire as she was lighting the stove.

Malini: Laxmi was never clumsy and we both know it. You identified the body. Was it . . . recognisable?

Anil: I don't want to talk about it.

Malini: There were people in the house when it happened. Couldn't anyone have prevented it?

Anil: Vinod tried to smother the flames with the living-room carpet. But it was too late.

Malini: That's another thing. The stove was in the kitchen. And she was found on the living-room floor.

Anil: She ran out in a panic . . . according to the evidence. These things happen, Malini.

Malini: Of course they do. All the time. Last year 350 women died of burns in this city alone, some of them over-insured wives.

Anil: What are you trying to say?

Malini: And when they died — plucked in their bloom by fiery fingers — the husband's family came into a lot of money.

Anil: For God's sake, the Marfatia family is in no need of money. And we don't even know that Laxmi was insured.

Malini: We do, as a matter of fact. Early this year. Laxmi told me so herself.

Anil: What you suggest is . . . horrible. I know Laxmi wasn't very happy in her marriage, but —

Malini: Not very happy! If I were given to hysterics, I'd laugh! They tormented and humiliated her because the dowry she brought them was not what they had angled for.

Anil: You know they didn't ask for a dowry. Their family business is thriving and they kept saying they wanted nothing from us.

Malini: But *we* know that those who protest too much are those who are greedy for plums! Not a day went by but her mother-in-law taunted Laxmi that Father had not honoured all his promises. And two sisters-in-law took up the chant that a goddess of wealth had entered their home with clothes fit for a servant and jewels not worth the name. And like a good son Vinod — chinless in more ways than one — joined the chorus because mama holds the purse strings!

Anil: Laxmi told you all this?

Malini: She was never the one to complain. I would have known nothing but for Tarla —

Anil: Who has a sweet tooth for gossip. As the only neighbour on the scene of the tragedy her testimony was vital, but she did not have much to say at the inquest today.

Malini: Perhaps she was scared to! *She* knew how they picked on Laxmi because in the five years there had been no children — as if Vinod couldn't be at fault there — and because she was the daughter of a retired clerk. . . Why did Father have to marry her into the family of vultures?

Anil: He thought he was doing his best for her. Look, she didn't have your advantages. She didn't make it to college — she didn't even quite complete her schooling —

Malini: Because with Mother always pregnant and ailing, she had to baby-sit for us! Laxmi was the brightest of us all. What right had Father to hold her back? It makes me sick, all this endless breeding and spawning —

Anil: He did what he could —

Malini: You keep saying that! But in five years her in-laws reduced her to — what? A cook? A menial — with all the heavy work they got out of her? A nullity, her nerves and pride shot to pieces? A stunt woman, her hurts and bruises a daily routine till finally they succeeded in —

Anil: Shut up! Stop it! I've had enough today, leave me alone.

Malini: No! Our sister is dead!

Anil: [*after a pause, during which Father coughs in his sleep*] Look, if there is a heavy insurance which Vinod's income cannot support —

Malini: Which is exactly what we need to find out —

Anil: — do you imagine the insurance company

17

does not investigate such claims before settling them? Let's stick to the facts, Malu. The thing was thoroughly investigated, a police panchnama was taken, five people gave evidence —

Malini: Which five? Vinod and his old bitch of a mother. Arjun, his fat slob of a brother. Kalu, their paid servant —

Anil: And Tarla, Laxmi's friend.

Malini: [*rounding on him*] You believe Laxmi's death was an accident?

Anil: You seriously believe her in-laws ringed round her and ignited her clothes?

Father: [*mumbling in his sleep, in the pause that follows Anil's question*] Lie still, lie still, or you will wake the children.

Anil: Come on, Malu. She is gone now. Let her go. She is beyond pain, beyond redress —

Malini: But not beyond retribution!

Anil: But what can we do? A court of law has —

Malini: I spit on your law courts! Playthings in the hands of exploiters and reactionaries, they deal out one kind of justice to the rich, another to the poor.

Anil: What kind of talk is this? From someone who's always wanted to go on to law college? Who's been feeding you on such catch phrases?

Malini: *Are* they? Roy says the law is only for those who can hire it to serve them — can you deny that?

Anil: Who is Roy?

Malini: Gita's husband — I've mentioned him before. He says even protection in uniform has its price — go and ask a Harijan. How many cases

18

of arson against them have reached the courts? I demand justice! That was my sister they set fire to.

Father: [*mumbling in his sleep*] Do they have cats' eyes that they can see in the dark? Lie still!

Anil: So what do you intend to do? What can you do?

Malini: I shall prowl among her neighbours, asking questions. Question the mother-in-law who with her tongue for a hatchet set about demolishing my sister. Question the servant. Question Arjun — an ice-cream cone should go a long way in loosening his tongue. Will you help me, Anil?

Anil: No.

Malini: Why not?

Anil: Because you've not convinced me. Because I have a new job to get on with.

Malini: Oh ho, a stupendous new job teaching spoilt brats all day for a pittance! You are wasted in that school and you know it. Why didn't you take up Sanjay's offer?

Anil: You know why.

Malini: No I don't. I thought he was a good friend.

Anil: [*with a shrug*] Sanjay applies only one test to everything he does: money and profits. Even at college he had a perfect measuring rod for everything: does it pay? — without a thought for the cost in human terms.

Malini: What has that to do with the job he's offered you? His father keeps indifferent health. One of these days he's going to die, and Sanjay

19

will be the supreme boss and you his right-hand man. . . Oh I agree that Sanjay tends to reduce quality to quantity and that like most successful businessmen there is something primitive about him . . . but that's what makes him so exciting.

Anil: Exciting?

Malini: Yes. To a woman. [*giving a nervous chuckle*] Don't worry, I know how to look after myself. [*defiantly*] I'm going out with him tonight. Don't ask me where.

Anil: I wasn't going to.

Malini: [*another nervous chuckle*] Perhaps I'll ask him to accompany me tomorrow when I impersonate Sherlock Holmes. . . Won't my sister's in-laws be impressed if I drive up with him in his Mercedes. . . [*quickly*] No they won't. They'll think I've taken to whoring.

Anil: If you said that to shock me —

Malini: [*hurrying*] So I shall go on foot and handcarry the evidence back. . . But I still don't know why you turned down Sanjay.

Anil: Then you haven't been listening. I'd also rather not work for the product his factory turns out.

Malini: For heaven's sake, it's only pesticides! You talk as if they were hand grenades.

Anil: And potentially as dangerous, unless the man controlling the production has . . . imagination. And compassion.

Malini: And Sanjay's something of a stampeder? Okay, but we need pesticides.

Anil: Yes we do. But when we compound substances unknown to nature, the long-term consequences of their use can be **dangerous. At** least unpredictable —

Malini: Oh Anil, can't you once, just once, be like everybody else? Because you have some kind of a romantic, utopian vision of work, you turned down a job with a four-figure salary? Why, Father could have paid up all debts incurred for Laxmi's wedding and used his pension as pocket money. And I could have lived in a style I'm so unused to, [*mockingly*] even improved my chances in the marriage market.

Anil: I'm sorry. It's important for me to be free to do what I want to do.

Malini: [*earnestly*] But freedom is money in the bank, Anil. You think if Laxmi had a fat bank account they could have trampled over her? Never. When I pass out next year I'm going to grab the job that gives me the fattest pay packet.

Anil: So, your dream of becoming another Portia has vanished like a pricked bubble! How sad that is.

Malini: I've decided that that dream would take too long. And I'm in a hurry.

Anil: To do what?

Malini: I've come to the conclusion that the weakness of democracies is that they move too slowly in the right direction.

Anil: And you want to move fast in the wrong direction?

Malini: Don't you get smart-ass with me!

Anil: All I'm trying to say is that you should work at what you like doing best.

Malini: Like you?

Anil: I'm happy doing what I am.

Malini: [*with bitter sarcasm*] Ah, the happiness of the poor. Their morals, their dignity and the way they keep up their tattered appearances — what shit! Look at this ugly room. That window with bars! Those cheap shiny calendars to hide the peeling plaster and exposed plumbing. And nothing on the stone floor but rolled bedding and a string bed, a chair with a sagging bottom and a table with rotting legs.

Anil: [*gently*] Aren't you forgetting that trunk there, prettied up with an old sari to look like a window seat?

Malini: [*pleased*] Oh, you think it looks pretty, Anil?

Anil: You've made an elegant job of it.

Malini: [*brusquely*] Nonsense. The poor have no taste: only hunger.

Anil: What do you keep in it, Malu? I've never seen you open it.

Malini: Secrets! Shotguns! You know, *bhaiya*, I feel if I can't live in the city's new skyscrapers I'd rather live on unmade roads in a low huddle of mud and tin and old boards than midways in middle-class, finger-pointing respectability. There I'd think myself lucky to have food, shelter, sex — with perhaps a latrine as a bonus. But right here I feel I'm under siege! I must have breathing space and books and fun and ideas and love and *beauty*! [*change of tone*] And you must have your tea, I suppose. [*moving towards the kitchen*]

22

Anil: [*stopping her*] Don't bother, Malu. It's too
          late for tea. Has Dad eaten?
Malini: No. His cough was bad all day and I
          couldn't even get him to swallow his medicine.
          See if he'll take something with you. I'm afraid
          the rice is burnt.
Anil: Again?
Malini: [*with a shrug*] When I am miserable I feel
          hungry, but it doesn't seem to improve my
          cooking—[*breaks off with a frown as she hears knocking
          on the front door*]
Anil: That must be Sanjay.
Malini: You know Sanjay never knocks like that,
          he blasts the bell. [*sharply, as Anil moves to open
          the door*] Wait. I'll open the door.
          [*Malini opens the door to admit* ROY, *thin as a rake,
          in black sweater and black pants, with an empty oversized
          canvas bag slung over his shoulder. There is something
          very alert about Roy — as if he's ready always to measure
          danger, to smell the wind like a jungle animal, to
          engage a foe*]
Roy: [*entering*] It's me and not the Boston
          Strangler, so don't stand there like a petrified
          chicken. [*with a sharp glance*] Why are you all
          dressed up?
Malini: [*under her breath*] I've told you never to
          call at this time. . . [*aloud*] My brother Anil.
          This is Roy. I don't think you've met.
Roy: [*measuring Anil, then insolently*] The school-
          teacher! No, I don't believe we have.
Anil: [*ironically*] The loss is mine —
Roy: I won't argue the point with you —
Anil: But one to which I'm already reconciled.

Father: [*who has stirred awake, pointing a shaking hand at Roy*] Vinod?

Roy: [*to Malini*] I was passing by and thought I'd pick up. . . [*pats his canvas bag*] those books.

Anil: What books?

Father: You have lost a lot of weight, Vinod. You've brought Laxmi with you?

Malini: [*sharply*] That's not Vinod, Dad.

Roy: [*to Anil*] A couple of books I had lent Malini to —

Malini: [*breaking in*] Shakespearian criticism. [*moves to the table*] I'll get them.

Roy: — to take her education in hand. My wife was grieved to hear about your sister. The inquest returned a verdict of accident?

Anil: Yes. How did you know?

Roy: I didn't. A logically inferred conclusion.

Father: What has happened to her? Where is Laxmi? In the kitchen?

Malini: Here! [*rushing up to Roy with two books, but dropping one in her nervousness. She moves to pick it up, but Anil is quicker*]

Anil: Allow me. [*reads the title*] The Anarchist Cookbook. One of Shakespeare's unpublished works?

Malini: That — those are a few recipes lent me by Gita. Give!

Anil: [*not relinquishing the book but turning it back to front*] Really? Stir together potassium nitrate, sulphur and wood-shavings in a saucepan. Serve cold and run away quickly. That sort of thing? [*to Roy*] Your wife must be an excellent cook. Unlike my sister.

Malini: Let me have it. [*she snatches it out of his hand and gives both books to Roy*] Thank her for me, will you?

Roy: I shall remember to do so.

Anil: [*neatly retrieving the second book from Roy's hand*] And this one is called *Murder and Liberty*. What recipes does this one list? Molotov cocktails? Shake up well together three parts of ferric oxide to one of aluminium powder —

Malini: Stop it.

Anil: [*reading*] By Karl Heinzen. Who is he? Master chef? Bartender?

Roy: [*in a deadly voice*] He was a German who wrote on terrorism and guerilla warfare and its political implications a hundred years before Mao Tse-tung.

Anil: I'm impressed.

Roy: If you had a taste for history —

Malini: [*quickly*] My brother teaches history at St. Paul's High School.

Roy: In that case you must have realised that murder on a colossal scale has been, and still is, the chief means of historical development.

Anil: No, I confess it never occurred to me to credit historical evolution to. . . assassins.

Roy: My thesis can be supported by an analysis of every revolution in history. Terrorism instils fear in the hearts of the oppressors —

Anil: That was also, I believe, the principal amusement of Genghis Khan.

Roy: — and gives courage to the oppressed of the world to achieve social and political ends.

Anil: Till in their turn, the victorious new classes

use terror to strike at dissent again?

Roy: The schoolteacher argues well. [*circling round Anil*] And now you would like to give us the quality of mercy speech?

Anil: Only if you think it will persuade you to rejoin the human race.

Malini: [*quickly, as if by rote*] Since reactionaries murder to maintain their rule, the revolutionist must murder to be free.

Anil: This is the second time tonight I've heard you mention "freedom". In two entirely different contexts, of course.

Father: [*mumbling*] It happened while lighting the stove. She must be taken to hospital at once. Her burns can be fatal. . . [*attempts to leave the chair*]

Anil: [*going to him*] Dad, there is no one in the kitchen.

Father: No one in the kitchen? [*befuddled*] She had such a light hand with her *puris* . . . The dough has to be just right. It's all in the dough. . .

Anil: Are you hungry, Dad?

Father: Yes, hungry. Yes, hungry. She — [*pointing an accusing finger at Malini*] gave me nothing to eat today.

Anil: Come, I'll warm up the food for you.

Roy: [*as Anil is helping Father to the kitchen*] My book, please!

Anil: Sure. [*throws the book at Roy, who catches it and unzips his canvas bag*] You have a lot of room in that for two books. [*exits with Father to the kitchen*]

Roy: He's quite sharp, your brother.

Malini: Roy, I told you never to call here when —

Roy: [*slaps the bag*] I brought this along on the chance that I'd be able to smuggle out the —

Malini: Under their noses? Are you mad?

Roy: [*enjoying her apprehension*] I thought you'd be only too happy to get rid of the incriminating evidence.

Malini: I would, too, but at this hour?

Roy: Evidently you are not ready for bed. [*looking her up and down*] Or are you?

Malini: [*whispering urgently*] Whenever I try to contact you, you've just left or are about to arrive or you're on your way to some place else — anything but there where you're needed!

Roy: [*with a grin*] That's called security. Relax. No one came snooping round my place, it was a false alarm. Actually, it was Gita's idea that I call on you on account of your sister. She would have come too, but she's not so well.

Malini: She does too much. Is it the fever again?

Roy: [*pause*] She's had an abortion.

Malini: [*shocked*] Oh I'm . . . I'm so sorry. How did it happen?

Roy: At a clinic.

Malini: At a . . .! I don't believe you. You mean she decided to — to get rid of it?

Roy: No. I did.

Malini: Roy! You know how much she wanted that baby —

Roy: I had warned her. This is not the time for breeding. She thought she could get away with

27

it. A *fait accompli* as they say in French —

Malini: You disgust me! Do you know that, Roy? You disgust me.

Roy: [*suddenly vicious*] Not as much as you disgust me! You think I don't know why you're all dressed up? Your sister's not been dead a few days —

Malini: Shut up! Shut up, Roy.

Roy: — and you are all dolled up to go sniffing after money, like all the others.

Malini: I forbid you to talk to me like that! He's rich, I know, but I love him, I can't help it.

Roy: Of course not. That's your instinct — to go sniffing after money with your pretty snout. You are in love with his pockets! They bulge with success.

Malini: Not true, not true.

Roy: You will lick his arse till he spits in your eye! You think Sanjay will ever marry a girl like you?

Malini: Why not?

Roy: Like hell he will! He will throw you crumbs from his table like you scatter feed corn for chicken. Or small change to a beggar.

Malini: I am no beggar!

Roy: No. You are a whore. Had I known it earlier, I would have taken you myself. That night, after I addressed the meeting and the hall was empty. . .

Malini: Get out, Roy. And don't ever come back.

Roy: No? So who will help you get rid of the dangerous little toys stashed up in this place. . . [*change of voice*] I'm sorry, Malini. I'm sorry, I'm sorry. It's just that. . . when I think of that bastard. . . You don't belong with him, don't you see?

Malini: Why? [*tears welling in her eyes*] Where do I belong? Where? [*turning away*] Don't you want me to be happy?

Roy: No. I never want happiness to swallow you up. You would be useless then. If you don't know what it is to seethe and cry and burst inside, why should you help us with our cause?

Malini: Yes! I suppose you would have to get someone else to do your dirty work.

Roy: [*blazing*] Dirty work! [*shaking her*] Dirty work! Don't you understand that we are engaged in a relentless struggle because we want a better deal for mankind? That what happened to your sister could not happen if —

Malini: If you mended the world with a few bomb blasts?

Roy: There is no remedy for the evils of our system except total destruction and a new beginning. Your sister —

Malini: Is well out of it! Let her be.

Roy: But are you going to spend the rest of your life like a child on a see-saw?

Malini: You want me to step down on to the killing-ground with you?

Roy: Malini, [*urgently*] you can't go back: go forward! Don't dream: act!

Malini: I will. I'm late for my date. [*picking up her handbag*] You can hang on here if you want to. [*raising her voice*] Anil? Anil I'm off. [*to Roy*] Perhaps women will stay at home every night

29

after the revolution? [*exits with a slam of the front door as Anil enters from the kitchen*]

Anil: She's left?

Roy: Flown the coop.

Anil: Alone?

Roy: [*sneering*] The prince did not call for her on a white charger, if that's what you mean. Not even in his yellow Mercedes.

[*Blackout, as they stare at each other*]

Act One
Scene 2

The same, a couple of hours later. FATHER *and* ANIL *are playing cards, the old man seated in his chair, Anil uncomfortably perched on the edge of the bed, with a stool between them.*

Father: [*cards in hand, peering down at the stool*] I want that ace!

Anil: All right, Dad. [*picking it up and giving it to him*]

Father: You know I pick up aces, yet you keep discarding them. You should pay more attention to the game, if you want to win. Come on.

Anil: You have to discard a card, Dad.

Father: I did.

Anil: No you didn't. Count the cards in your hand.

Father: All right. [*discards a card with an unsteady hand*] Rummy is not entirely a game of chance, you know. You have to use your head. [*as Anil plays his hand*] Vinod didn't stay long, did he?

Anil: That wasn't Vinod, Father.

Father: Is that a jack of spades?

Anil: Yes.

Father: I want it. Rummy! Three times in succession. There. [*putting his cards down on the stool*] What are you looking at? You think I've

31

cheated? [*mixing up the cards quickly*] My deal this time. [*with trembling fingers collects the cards, Anil helping him, then tries to deal*] He was not Vinod? Then why didn't you tell me at the time?

Anil: Let me do that for you, Dad. [*firmly takes the pack away from Father and deals*] This will be the last game. I have a lot of correction books to go through for school tomorrow.

Father: You teach mathematics?

Anil: History, Father. [*he's finished dealing*] All tens are jokers. Right. I begin.

Father: You dealt the cards, so I begin.

Anil: I dealt them on your behalf, Dad. So I — All right, you begin.

Father: I want that queen! [*Anil gives it to him*] Years ago I read somewhere that death by fire is quicker than it seems. [*mumbling*] Yes, quicker than it seems.

Anil: You have to reject a card.

Father: Fire eats up oxygen. . .

Anil: Throw down a card, Dad.

Father: Most people die quickly of suffocation. . .

Anil: [*sharply*] Your card!

Father: . . . and not of burns. [*throws down a card*] But the dead take a longer time. I remember putting the torch to my father's mouth, as his eldest son. . . on the day we cremated him. . .

Anil: [*playing*] It's your turn again.

Father: [*playing shakily*] It took a long time before the skull exploded.

Anil: Hold your cards with both your hands, or they'll fall.

Father: [*obeying*] He was a big man with anger in him. . . used to beat me up for no reason. . . [*sharply*] What are you doing?

Anil: Picking up the eight you discarded.

Father: The eight was not on top!

Anil: Yes it was.

Father: How? When I just played the king? You pay no attention! Even as a boy I tried to teach you cards, but you never learnt! [*mumbling*] I educated all of you. Used to work overtime, because I did not know how to hold out my palm under the table like the others — I was scared to. Slaved on holidays even. . . to send you to good schools. What's that card now?

Anil: Nine of hearts.

Father: Don't want it. Never got to be the Head Clerk. I was forgotten by my bosses — by everyone. Even by your mother, after you were born.

Anil: Your turn.

Father: [*suddenly childlike in his anxiety*] I don't hold it against you, Anil, you mustn't think that. Don't know what I'd do without you now that Laxmi. . . [*pauses blankly*] She's in the kitchen?

Anil: [*throwing down his cards*] For God's sake!

Father: [*trembling*] The dead take a long time to burn. You have to feed them with ghee to help the flames along —

Anil: Dad —

Father: Anything I did, I did for her good!

Anil: I know —

Father: [*struggling up in his chair*] They let her burn, they let us burn, my daughter. . . [*hoarsely, almost weeping*] The swine, the swine. . .

33

Anil: [*struggling with him*] Sit down, Dad. Sit down, sit down.

[*There is a loud ring of the door bell*]

Father: [*freezing*] That must be her!

Anil: Sit down, for God's sake, and let me see to the door. Who — [*opens the door to admit PROFESSOR PALKAR, a short overweight man in his fifties, with sharp eyes and a pugnacious jaw*] Oh. Please come in, Sir. I never expected —

Palkar: [*out of breath*] To see me still alive and kicking, eh? With one foot in the grave years ago?

Anil: I mean that you should not have taken the trouble, Sir. The stairs are rather steep. Meet my father. Dad, this is Professor Palkar, with whom I studied history at the university.

Palkar: Namasté!

Father: [*staring vaguely*] Who?

Anil: But please take a seat. [*pulls out the chair from against the table and removes the books from it*] Can I get you something to drink?

Palkar: [*sitting on chair and mopping his brow*] No, thank you. I hear that my star pupil has become a pedagogue himself, though I tried my best to head him off into a less heroic profession. [*judiciously*] You are a fool, Anil.

Anil: [*with a grin*] You always said so, Sir.

Palkar: I meant it each time.

Anil: I admit that teaching rich men's pampered kids is not really my scene. I would have preferred to work with a different set of children. In a little village school-cum-workshop.

Palkar: Yes? But in most of our villages children

are hired out in the fields after their eighth year.

Anil: But that's just what I would like to change. Because —

Palkar: You are an imbecile if you believe you can change anything in this country. Life goes on, the past continues. Read your history. After every conquest and destruction the past simply reasserted itself.

Anil: As I see it, with the transmission of new ideas and new work opportunities at village level —

Palkar: Rubbish. You cannot teach the new because you cannot dislodge the old. The villager has fixed ideas in his head. Not ideas with which he thinks, mind you, or which are in any way the result of judgement, but obsessions which have seeped into his mind and damned him to a thousand years of stagnation and defeat. [getting up excitedly, as if delivering a lecture] And what are these obsessions? One: his caste.

Anil: If I may be permitted to say, Sir —

Palkar: Two: his belief in karma, the Hindu excuse for all failures. The self-cherishing distortion that makes him see history as a religious fable!

Anil: But perhaps without this belief to sustain him he could not bear his misery?

Palkar: Bah! Can you change a people who accept misery as the condition of man? In their very abjectness lies their security. They don't want change.

Anil: But with education —

Father: [*mumbling*] I educated all my children . . .
          all . . .

Palkar: [*excitedly*] Nothing will change us! Don't
          you see, that is why culturally we preserve and
          we repeat. Artistically, too. Even when we appear
          to create, we only imitate, we borrow, we
          plagiarise — at best we give modern twists to
          ancient concepts. For instance, even today the
          widow is expected to achieve virtue, to secure
          the honour of her husband's family by a self-
          effacement as total as when she burned herself
          on her lord's funeral pyre —

Father: [*mumbling wild-eyed*] They let her burn,
          they let her burn!

Palkar: [*brought to earth*] Forgive me for running
          off at a tangent — like I do so often in the
          classroom.

Father: [*mumbling*] Cruel, godless men. Cruel . . .
          [*head sinks sideways, he falls asleep*]

Anil: It's all right. He's fallen asleep.

Palkar: It was sad business and a great blow to
          him. [*sitting*] Incidentally, Dr. Ram Lodha, who
          attended your sister that evening, is a personal
          friend of mine. You only have to give him my
          name if you wish to see him. [*abruptly*] Was
          there a suicide note?

Anil: [*startled*] What do you mean, Sir? The
          inquest today returned a verdict of accident.

Palkar: [*too quickly*] Yes of course.

Anil: Was it something Dr. Lodha told you that
          makes you suspect the existence of such a note?
          You may be frank with me, Sir.

Palkar: Not at all, not at all. [*pause*] Ram did mention, however, that your sister had been dead three and a half hours when they sent for him.

Anil: Vinod said they tried to reach him earlier, but he could not be contacted.

Palkar: Well, it was sad business, very sad. I am truly sorry.

Anil: Malini gave me your note, Sir. It was kind of you to also call in person —

Palkar: [*standing up*] Is your sister at home?

Anil: No.

Palkar: Good. I can talk freely. Malini is not in my class but doing well at her work, I hear. . . But I doubt the friends she has chosen are very good for her.

Anil: What do you mean, Sir?

Palkar: Oh I know students are a discontented lot today, there is a great sense of betrayal among them and with reason. Their numbers are escalating, the institutions are overcrowded — ballooned far beyond their capacity to educate — and at the end of it all, where are the jobs? In the growing frustration the general attitude is, "Why bother to graduate, when we are only going to swell the ranks of the unemployed?"

Anil: But you said Malini is doing well at her work.

Palkar: [*sharply*] I'm saying that there is a breeding ground for terrorism in the disarray of our education system!

Anil: And Malini is involved with an aggrieved student group, Sir?

Palkar: With an aggrieved and politicised group, Anil. Unemployed or poorly employed ex-students, wedded to a radical ideology, foment violence on campuses and outside. [*abruptly*] Something happened which has disturbed me very much. I must talk about it.

Anil: Please feel free to do so, Sir.

Palkar: It started last month with a burst pipe in the ceiling of my flat. I complained to the landlord about the seepage of water in my drawing-room; then, when he did nothing, took my complaint to the municipality. On Monday last firemen and police forced their way into the locked apartment above me. We found, among other things, eight automatic pistols, a sawn-off shotgun, ten fake or stolen auto licences, a hand grenade and some pamphlets and books . . . On the flyleaf of one of the books was inscribed the name, Roy Mukherjee. What's the matter? You know him?

Anil: I've . . . met him.

Palkar: He passed out of the university at least seven years ago and I thought he was in Calcutta, where I heard he had married a Bengali girl. But recently I've seen him hanging around your sister. Once outside the university gates. Once I saw them jump out of a taxi on to a moving bus! Tell her to stay away from him. He is a trouble-maker.

Anil: You say the police have his name. What are they doing?

Palkar: Keeping an eye on him, hoping he'll lead them to bigger things. I must go now. It's late.

[*at the door where Anil has accompanied him*] Where is Malini at this late hour?

Anil: She's . . . visiting a friend.

Palkar: Tell her to be careful how she chooses her friends. [*pause*] I've been receiving threatening notes by mail. . . slogans are chalked on the blackboard in my class . . . A hoodlum on a motorbike almost ran me over twice this week, as I crossed the streets. . . [*wryly*] Obviously they think I'm the informer who led the police to their secret hideout when they were betrayed by a leaking pipe! Well, I must be off.

Anil: Wait, Sir! I'll see you home. [*a quick glance over his shoulder at Father*] I'll be back before he knows it —

Palkar: You will do nothing of the sort. Do I look weak on my pins?

Anil: No, but I'd rather you didn't walk back alone —

Palkar: You'll stay where you are! Remember me to your sister when she comes in and look after her. . . Sometimes the shock of a violent end can push one into embracing an extremist philosophy —

Anil: Not Malini. Her impulses are too warm and generous, and she has this — this hunger for beauty.

Palkar: But intellectually she is still experimenting, remember that.

Anil: [*with a smile*] Above all she is still Cinderella, sighing for her rags to turn into riches, her pumpkin into a shiny Mercedes. . . Good night, Sir. Thank you — and take care.

[*Anil closes the door after Palkar and stands leaning against it, deep in thought. Then he walks to the table, picks up the set of exercise books as if to begin his correction work, then drops them and quickly walks back to the front door. He opens it and stands there, irresolute, as if deciding to go after Palkar or not. Shrugs, closes the door. On his way back to pick up the exercise books, he stubs his toe against the trunk, so severely, that he hops in pain, then sits on it, nursing his toe. As the pain subsides he feels, with his hands, the surface he is seated on*]

Anil: [*as his fingers encounter a lock*] She never locked this trunk before! [*He frowns, gets up, hobbles to the kitchen. Returns with an iron poker. He draws back the cloth covering the trunk and, wielding the poker, bursts open the lock, glancing back every now and then to see if the noise wakes up Father, who sleeps through it all. At last he slides back the open bolt and the heavy lid yawns open protestingly. He squats before the trunk painfully and quickly removes from it worn towels, used pillow-cases, a couple of old bedsheets, old books, a pair of old sandals wrapped in newspaper, a soft pile of sari petticoats. Then abruptly he stands up, gazing down with an expression of shocked disbelief on his face.*] God, what has Malu got herself into! Firearms!

[*Bending over, he picks out of the trunk a helmet and a cosh. Then three pistols and finally a shotgun. Blackout, as Anil is handling the shotgun gingerly, his head bowed over it.*]

Act One

Scene 3

MALINI *is seated on the sofa in Sanjay's sumptuous living-room, a thick rug at her feet. The time is after 10 p.m.* SANJAY, *cigarette in hand, is prowling round, his manner impatient, disgruntled.*

Malini: What's the matter? You told me you had settled the strike at the plant — so now why does the reigning prince of industry look so peeved?

Sanjay: Damn it! First you keep me waiting all evening —

Malini: Why didn't you offer to come and fetch me, Sanjay? You know I have to perform feats of ballet to avoid having my bottom pinched at that crowded bus-stop.

Sanjay: — then you say you are not spending the night!

Malini: I can't because I told Anil I was meeting you.

Sanjay: Why did you? You usually tell him you're spending the night at a girlfriend's. Have you suddenly decided to embrace sanyas?

Malini: Don't be ridiculous. I have things on my mind, I told you.

Sanjay: So if you're on a thinking jag, why come here at all? Let me take you home. Come on, get up!

Malini: [*stretching*] I'm very comfortable here, thank you, so don't be such a grouch. This a new rug? I don't remember seeing it before. Gorgeous. My feet sink into it like grass. Must have cost you enough to feed a working-class family for — six months?

Sanjay: Depends on the size of the working-class family. They breed like cats and dogs.

Malini: Yes they do, don't they? They are monsters of fecundity. [*abruptly*] My friend's had an abortion. Gita.

Sanjay: I thought you said she was married.

Malini: Of course she is! They live nine to a room. There's Roy, his parents, his brother, his wife and their three children — you can imagine the squeeze.

Sanjay: Wait a minute. You're talking of Roy Mukherjee? Gita's *his* wife? I wouldn't see much of them, if I were you. This Roy has a mean and hungry look.

Malini: Where did you meet him? Not at a cocktail bar or a golf course, I bet.

Sanjay: He came to me for a job.

Malini: And you didn't give it to him?

Sanjay: I had the good sense not to. They think he's behind the Nagpur derailment, which killed twenty people. The police are keeping tabs. [*sitting on the rug at her feet*] Slip down here on the rug with me, Malu love.

Malini: How do you know?

Sanjay: What?

Malini: You have friends in the police? Don't answer that one, Sanjay. People in your position

42

have a smooth network of appropriate connections. Are they going to nab him?

Sanjay: Roy? If they can pin anything on him, yes. What a small foot you have. It fits into my palm.

Malini: Roy believes in a better future for mankind. Is that a crime?

Sanjay: No, but mass murder is.

Malini: If one wants to accomplish the end, one must not flinch from the means. . . Believe it or not, Sanjay, I have a streak of violence in me.

Sanjay: Oh I believe it! In fact, there are scratches on my back to prove it. Join me down here, Malu. What lovely legs you have. Mmm, smooth as silk. Suddenly I'm in the mood for —

Malini: Let go! What do you think you're doing?

Sanjay: [*softly*] I thought, sweetie, your interest lay in the performing arts — oouch! That almost landed on my nose!

Malini: My foot will behave if you keep your hands to yourself.

Sanjay: And flinch from the means? Come on, baby, let me practise what you preach. All's fair in love and war —

Malini: I don't know about love, but the way we all live is only a stone's throw from warfare. Except for my brother —

Sanjay: Your brother is a crank! I'm very fond of Anil, but you must admit he's still wet behind the ears. Imagine working like a dhobi's ass all day for a piddling salary when he could have started on three times that with me!

Malini: People like Anil only seem naive and you think they can be baited. . . Then it turns out that they have the good sense and we are the fools. From schooldays my brother walked off with all the prizes.

Sanjay: Okay, so he's goddam brilliant. Which doesn't make him less pigheaded.

Malini: I've always been a pretty good student myself. There's talk of my taking up law when I pass out — if I can do that along with a job. It will be tough going, I suppose, but Anil's prepared to help, and there are scholarships. Oh yes, *I* can win prizes too, if you'd like to know.

Sanjay: I know: you have a trophy at your feet. But what's Anil got? Except for a bee in his bonnet about starting a school in some god-forsaken village? Even came to see my old man for some financial assistance from the Company for his asinine scheme.

Malini: [*sitting up, interested*] Anil didn't tell me that. What did your father say?

Sanjay: Poured cold water on such idiocy, of course — but in the same breath offered him a job! On the spot, mind you, and Father's a tough nut to crack.

Malini: And Anil refused?

Sanjay: You know your brother, what do you think? Can you tell me what that fathead has against the factory? What his bellyache is about? We have 250 men on our rolls — isn't that the idea, technology that can create employment for the poor buggers?

Malini: Anil believes you don't care for the

people you employ — or even the goods you produce: but only what you can gain from them. The workers are an item of cost you'd reduce to a minimum, if you could. And that's what you're aiming at, aren't you, now that the strike is over?

Sanjay: But this is crazy! As a private individual I may be interested in goodness, truth, beauty and all that crap, but certainly as a businessman I concern myself with profits. How can a business run without profits?

Malini: Which means the rich will continue to be rich and the poor to be poor — precisely because those who have nothing to sell but their labour are in the worst possible bargaining position. Anil finds such a set-up inhuman.

Sanjay: So he wants me to hold their hands? What does he want? [*waxing indignant*] What the hell does he want?

Malini: Hey, this argument is between you two, remember? — so leave me out of it.

Sanjay: [*exploding*] He's a fool! A nitwit! His hang-up is that he is infected with romantic doubts about the industrial civilisation — doubts which only rich countries can afford to footle around with. And they are romantic because nobody in his senses wants to give up the fruits of his enterprise. . . Your brother needs to have his head examined! You know what the stick-in-the-mud sat there and said to my father?

Malini: Tell me.

Sanjay: Hell, I wouldn't remember all of it. But he leaned across the desk to Pop and asked

45

him — very politely, of course — why financial adventurers like him should be allowed to entice hordes of villagers into crowded slums — entice, mind you! — assume no responsibility for the conditions created, and fling them into destitution once their usefulness was over. . .? He said some more, too, a whole mouthful, then bowed to my father — who was rather dazed by it all — and left. I always suspected Anil was a goddam crank. Now I also know he's a pain in the ass.

Malini: [*rather smugly*] Oh well, my brother happens to believe that education should not be a passport to privilege.

Sanjay: [*exploding again*] So every graduate student should take a kind of monastic vow to serve the people? A bloody sacred oath or something?

Malini: Why not? When I become a lawyer I mean to work for women's causes. . . redress their wrongs. . . help break their chains.

Sanjay: [*mocking*] Such a heroic resolve!

Malini: I'm serious, Sanjay.

Sanjay: You're as crazy as your brother! Do you know Anil even tried to interest me in his village scheme. Can you imagine me in a village?

Malini: No.

Sanjay: Not on your life. All those small fields, ragged men sunk in vegetative decay, huts and mud and mosquitoes — not for me. Not even if all the girls there have tanned titties and are willing. Come and try this magic carpet with me, Malu. It's soft, it's warm, it turns me on.

Malini: Not tonight, Sanjay. I'm doubled up like a fist. . . I told you the inquest today returned a verdict of accident.

Sanjay: So?

Malini: I'm pretty sure Laxmi's death was not an accident.

Sanjay: So what do you think it was? Murder? Martyrdom?

Malini: [*getting up*] I don't know. Five people gave evidence, but three of those five used to gang up on her and make her life a misery.

Sanjay: So what are you trying to say? They schemed and plotted the destruction of your sister? Let me tell you that Vinod is not such a bad chap. He is known in the business world —

Malini: [*with contempt*] Business world! You mean there's honour among thieves?

Sanjay: Look, damn it, I've met him. In fact he came to see me on an errand of mercy.

Malini: Vinod? We can't be speaking of the same person.

Sanjay: Shut up and listen. There's this chap employed with us in the sales department — a wastrel, a chronic absentee. With a few drinks under his belt he's foul-mouthed, quarrelsome. Early this month I fired him. Well, it turned out that he is a neighbour of Vinod's and Vinod called on me in person to reinstate him. Said the chap's wife and daughter were starving.

Malini: [*in a strange voice*] And you did?

Sanjay: Sure. Always do a businessman a favour. You never know when you'll need one in return —

Malini: [*getting up*] Vinod's neighbour, you said?

Sanjay: Well, they still live in that crummy old building in Bhuleshwar. Vinod told me — and I guess you know — that they're planning to move out as soon as their new flat is ready. . . What's up with you?

Malini: The name of this neighbour. Is it Gadgil?

Sanjay: Suresh Gadgil. Hell, how do you know?

Malini: Tarla's husband! That's why, at the inquest, she said nothing.

Sanjay: What are you babbling about?

Malini: [*agitated*] Tarla was there when it happened. When Laxmi burned to death. She was Laxmi's friend, she knew how my sister was abused and bullied, but it wasn't the story she gave out in court. Why?

Sanjay: I don't know. You tell me.

Malini: Because Vinod came to you and got her husband reinstated in his job. She was obliged to Vinod, don't you see, so she kept her mouth shut about what happened.

Sanjay: What did happen?

Malini: That I mean to find out.

Sanjay: You ought to be with the CID.

Malini: [*wringing her hands*] I knew it, I knew it, my poor sister.

Sanjay: [*going to her*] God, you're obsessed with this thing! Paranoid! [*puts his arms round her*] You'll make yourself sick, Malu.

Malini: [*pulling away*] Don't you see, don't you see, we were up against a smooth wall of deception and this is the first crack my fingers have encountered? They will find others.

Sanjay: Forget it, Malu. [*holding her again*] Let me

help you forget.

Malini: My head hurts so —

Sanjay: Because you fasten on an idea with a dog's fangs! Relax. [*whispering*] Get out of your things, Malu, and come and lie with me on the rug. [*tugging at her sari*] You can feel its caress on your bare skin. . . there's nothing like it, I promise you.

Malini: [*pulling away*] No. Stop it.

Sanjay: Stop being such an ass-aching Puritan.

Malini: Don't you tear my sari, you brute.

Sanjay: I'll buy you another one. I'll shower you with chiffons!

Malini: More flimsy promises? Or a fringe benefit, like the *Levis* you bought Mrs. Lobo? How *is* the frisky Mrs. Lobo these days?

Sanjay: Her shorthand is getting worse and worse.

Malini: Nobody could accuse her of brains. But her other aptitudes?

Sanjay: Not a patch on yours.

Malini: Shut up! How dare you compare me to her? [*in despair*] I'm not given to easy infidelities, but how would you know?

Sanjay: You brought up the subject. You know I'm not in the least interested in Thelma Lobo.

Malini: But she is momentarily deranged about you.

Sanjay: For which I am not to blame.

Malini: But she was here with you last night? On that rug?

Sanjay: [*turning away to light a cigarette*] Let's not quarrel about this again, Malini.

Malini: Let's not! But let's know how we stand

in relation to each other, right?

Sanjay: I think I better drive you home.

Malini: No. I want to talk. I want to know where I stand with you, Sanjay.

Sanjay: What is there to know?

Malini: God, I never thought I'd ask you this. But after what happened to Laxmi. . . I must know which road to take. Are you going to marry me?

Sanjay: [*evasively*] You know my father is old. A heart patient. He's done a hell of a lot for us — he started this business almost from scratch, amassed his wealth in a lifetime. . . So now there's pressure on me to — to. . . think of marriage ties with the right family.

Malini: [*from a tight throat*] I see. Someone on the same guest lists and clubs and charities. . . Don't say any more, please Sanjay.

Sanjay: I've always had the use of money, but after Dad I'll have the control of it. . . and responsibilities towards the next generation.

Malini: [*with a shrill laugh*] So the pesticides prince will marry a textiles princess? And even their horoscopes will tally and she will be a virgin.

Sanjay: All right, Malini, I'm taking you home.

Malini: And the two bloodlines will prosper dramatically. And your children will be little satraps with all of life served up on silver platters — good fortune locked up in their very genes! How neatly these things are managed! Congratulations, Sanjay.

Sanjay: Hell, this doesn't mean I'm going to give you up. God knows you are in my blood,

Malu —

Malini: [*choking on a sob*] Oh I know! It's true love. The real thing!

Sanjay: — and I mean to look after you. Soon as you've passed out I'll give Thelma the sack. You can forget your claptrap about being a lawyer and come in to work for me. Haven't you always said, what's the use of living in the jet age if you have no money for the tickets? As my secretary, we can travel everywhere together —

Malini: Shut up, shut up, shut up!

Sanjay: What are you so sore about? Listen, I think I can get away from work a couple of hours tomorrow. Let's meet here again before lunch and we'll sort this out.

Malini: No. Tomorrow I have an engagement.

Sanjay: Cancel it. Is it so bloody important?

Malini: Life and death. I must find out about Laxmi.

Sanjay: I told you these things are best forgotten. Be reasonable, Malu —

Malini: [*intensely*] You couldn't hold me back with a mule's harness.

Sanjay: You could never keep your fingers off a scab, that's your problem.

Malini: I have to complete a jigsaw, a crossword, find my way through a maze. . . [*fighting her hysteria*] Isn't it funny, Sanjay, that with a fat dowry Laxmi would have been a flaming success overnight — instead of a heap of ashes today? Doesn't it make you laugh?

Sanjay: Stop that! You've been impossible all evening.

Malini: I feel I'm falling — falling. . . Sanjay.

Sanjay: To hell with you! [*throwing away his cigarette*] I'll see you home.

Malini: No! Let's get down on that rug. . . my emergency landing strip.

Sanjay: You're joking.

Malini: Try me.

Sanjay: [*greedily*] You — you can't mean it, Malu love?

Malini: After which I shall begin the self's spring-cleaning, some dreadful exorcism to undo the defilement. . . [*with growing desperation*] perhaps just one powerful act of contrition — who knows?

Sanjay: [*thickly*] Come on, come on Malu, get out of all this. . . I have a mad need of you. . . there's a wolf in me tonight. . . [*his hands are all over her*]

Malini: [*very still*] Or do you think self-loathing *is* a kind of purity?

[*Curtain as he continues to undress her. End of Act One*]

Act Two

Scene 1

Early next morning. MALINI *is in her tenement room (same as Act One, Scene 1) with* FATHER. *He is seated in his usual chair, cup of tea in hand.*

Father: The tea is cold again. [*slurping it*] And your eyes are all red. [*slurp*]

Malini: I'll warm it for you. Give!

Father: She used to make a lovely cup of tea. Sujata. I hate cold tea. [*drinking*] Why did Anil leave so early this morning?

Malini: I don't know, I told you. He left before I was awake.

Father: You like to sleep late, [*slurp*] that's why your eyes are so swollen. He left in the dark. Why do they work him so hard at the school?

Malini: He couldn't have left for school at 5 o'clock in the morning!

Father: With a suitcase full of books. My mathematics teacher wrote out sums on the blackboard from his head. He needed no books.

Malini: [*wearily*] Anil does not teach maths, Father. [*sharply*] What books? The exercise books he brought home for correction are still on the table — [*breaks off as Anil enters from the front door, carrying a battered suitcase*] Anil! Where on earth have you been?

53

Anil: [*evading her eyes*] I must rush if I'm to be in time for school. You think you can help me find a fresh shirt, Malini? [*he drops the suitcase on the bed*]

Malini: Of course. And your bath water?

Anil: No time.

Malini: [*as she reaches for a shirt on the clothes peg*] What's in the suitcase?

Anil: It's empty now.

Malini: But where have you been? I have so much to tell you, Anil. Do you know why Tarla kept a close guard on her tongue at the inquest —

Anil: If you won't hurry, I'll miss the assembly bell. [*removes shirt over his head*]

Malini: [*picking it up and handing him a fresh one*] This is soaking wet — as if you've been running.

Anil: I went on an errand.

Malini: Shall I pack your lunch? And get you your milk — [*moves towards the kitchen*]

Father: My tea was cold again. Every day it is cold.

Anil: [*to Malini*] Leave it be! I have no time.

Father: [*mumbling*] She used to take pains to please me. Sujata. [*he starts coughing and Malini rescues the cup from his hand*]

Malini: [*to Anil*] You should at least have a cup of milk before —

Anil: [*shouting, as she turns towards the kitchen again*] I don't want it, I told you! [*as she stops in astonishment at his tone*] You might as well know. Palkar's had a heart attack. It's serious this time.

Malini: Palkar?

Anil: Professor Palkar at the university.

Malini: Oh. [*she deposits the cup on the table*] Is that why you rushed out early —

Anil: [*almost shouting again*] I left on an errand! [*calming himself*] On my way back I passed his house and something made me look him up. He lives alone. His neighbours had called his doctor. [*pause*] Dr. Ram Lodha.

Malini: The same doctor who attended on Laxmi?

Anil: The same. Palkar was heavily sedated, but I had a talk with Dr. Lodha while they were awaiting the ambulance. They're taking him to the Bhatia Hospital.

Malini: I'm sorry. Professor Palkar was so kind when he heard about Laxmi. Called me after class, gave that note for you —

Anil: He came to see me last night.

Malini: He did? Here?

Anil: After you left. Kick my shoes out. [*she bends to pull them out from under the bed, as he wears them*] Quite late. [*in sudden anguish*] I should have walked him back, I should have walked him back!

Malini: Why, what difference would that have made? He's had a heart problem for years —

Anil: [*tying his shoelaces*] One of the neighbours' boys saw him being roughed up on the street last night, almost on his own doorstep. Raju shouted from his window, then ran down three flights of stairs. The toughs — there were two of them — drove away on their motorbike, and Palkar was brought up unconscious to his room.

55

Malini: How dreadful! Had he been robbed?

Anil: No. Just kicked around. An old man!

Malini: The beasts. I'll go round to the hospital later, Anil. But please listen to what I've learnt about Tarla's husband —

Anil: Another time.

Malini: No, now! He works for Sanjay, but he's a quarrelsome drunken bum who cannot keep a job and when he was fired from his last position it was Vinod who got him reinstated. Vinod!

Anil: [*moving to the table*] I've got my wallet on me. Must remember to take the books.

Malini: [*following him*] Are you listening? Can't you see what this means? We now know why Tarla was obliged to keep her mouth shut about what she knew. [*holding him by the arm*] You must speak to Vinod today, confront him with this thing, challenge him about the insurance policy in Laxmi's name —

Anil: [*flinging off her hand*] The man I want to speak to today is Roy!

Malini: Roy! What's Roy got to do with —

Anil: Plenty! Now you listen to me. Palkar's complaint about a leaking pipe in his ceiling led the authorities to investigate the vacant flat above his, and they stumbled on to a terrorist hideout —

Malini: Oh no!

Anil: Oh yes! Palkar innocently reported a burst pipe and they took him to be an informer, an enemy of the people — isn't that the phrase? So they tried to instil terror into him by slogans chalked on his blackboard —

Malini: Anil, I swear I know nothing —

Anil: By breaking his window panes with stones, by threatening letters in the post and by trying to run him over with a motorbike . . . an old man with a weak heart!

Malini: Who are "they"?

Anil: That's one of the questions I'm going to put to Roy.

Malini: Why Roy? I don't think Roy had anything to do with it —

Anil: I have no time to argue, Malini, but my advice to you is not to let Roy come anywhere near you. [*opens the front door on his way out*]

Malini: [*shouting after him*] Anil! Please see Vinod today, please. This is the first crack in the wall I was looking for. We will find others! They killed our sister!

[*Blackout*]

Act Two
Scene 2

VINOD *is seated in his office, looking lost behind his large desk because he is a small man with a round, petulant face and a diminutive chin. The phone on his desk rings. Vinod takes time to look up from his paperwork, then picks up the receiver.*

Vinod: [*speaking into his phone, voice surly*] Yes? Who! What does he want?. . . Brother-in-law or no brother-in-law, tell him Vinod Marfatia does not see anyone without appointment. . . Okay, so you give him an appointment for next week, tell him I'll see him next week. [*bangs down the phone; it promptly rings again. Vinod snatches up the receiver, peevishly*] Now what is it? [*sitting up*] What the — ? Now you listen to me, Anil, I'm busy, and the girl just told you I don't see — What! Now look here, if you don't want to be thrown out. . . What do you mean, for my own good. . . All right, damn it. . . You can — hello, hello?
  [*But Anil has evidently called off, and as Vinod replaces the receiver, Anil enters the office*]
Vinod: [*self-importantly*] Yes, Anil? Next time you will not be allowed to barge in without an appointment. These are business hours and I'm expecting an important client in five minutes. Is there something you wanted?

58

Anil: Not to trespass on your time, I'll come straight to the point: what was the amount for which Laxmi's life was insured?

Vinod: [*after a startled hush*] What — what is all this about? We owe you nothing!

Anil: I'm instituting a further inquiry into Laxmi's accident. I can get this information from other sources, if you are not willing to give it to me.

Vinod: You people want to create trouble, is that it? But don't forget there's been a *pucca* investigation of the case and you heard the coroner's verdict yesterday.

Anil: I am not satisfied with the verdict. [*turning to go*] You'll be hearing from me.

Vinod: Wait! Sit down, Anil. I know this has been very upsetting for all of us. . . What I've been through no one can guess.

Anil: [*remains standing*] I can see, Vinod, that you are inconsolable.

Vinod: Look here. And here. These are burns on my hands as I tried to beat down the flames — and you've been listening to people advising you to rake up the whole painful matter again! What do you hope to gain by it?

Anil: Justice. There are certain vital questions that were not raised at the inquest, certain incongruities that were not explained.

Vinod: Really? Such as?

Anil: [*sitting*] Such as why no doctor was summoned till three and a half hours after Laxmi's death.

Vinod: Damn it, the kitchen fire was spreading, the — the place was an inferno, yet I called Dr.

Lodha before I called the fire brigade — but he was out!

Anil: I thought it was a neighbour who sent for the fire brigade.

Vinod: What difference who sent for it? The point is a doctor was summoned at the earliest possible —

Anil: When you were told on the phone that Dr. Lodha was out, did you leave a message for him?

Vinod: [*a slight hesitation*] I must have. [*more confidently*] Of course I left a message!

Anil: Who with?

Vinod: With his wife or compounder or somebody, how do I remember now?

Anil: You rang up Dr. Lodha at home?

Vinod: He works at home! His clinic is a room set apart in his flat — Look, I don't have to answer your bloody —

Anil: I find it strange that when you couldn't get Dr. Lodha you didn't try other doctors.

Vinod: Who said I didn't?

Anil: And they were all unavailable?

Vinod: Yes! For one reason or another, which I [*sarcastic*] didn't have the time to note in my diary! It happens sometimes.

Anil: When did you finally contact Dr. Lodha?

Vinod: When he didn't show up, we had to send Kalu for him. After the fire was put out.

Anil: Yet when the fire brigade arrived, you sent it back because the fire was already out. What time was that?

Vinod: Look here, you cheeky bastard, give me

one good reason why I should sit here answering your —

Anil: The post mortem clearly established that my sister's death occurred between 7.15 and 7.30 p.m. And the fire must have been put out well before 8, because that's when you sent the fire brigade back. Yet you did not send Kalu for Dr. Lodha till almost 11 at night. Why?

Vinod: I told you, damn it! I'd left a message for him. Several messages!

Anil: Not one of which he received?

Vinod: His wife must have forgotten to give them to him.

Anil: You are a liar, Vinod.

Vinod: [*springing up*] You have the gall to barge in on me in my own office and call me —

Anil: You are a liar, Vinod. You did not leave a message with Dr. Lodha's wife because that Tuesday she happened to be out of town. Nor could you have spoken to the compounder because he was sick that day and did not report for work at all.

Vinod: So it could have been his servant I spoke to! His children! Could have been —

Anil: Sit down and listen. Dr. Lodha's last patient left at 7 that Tuesday evening, and because he was alone in the flat he worked late at his desk where the phone is, but there was no message from you at all, till Kalu came for him.

Vinod: [*subsiding in his chair*] How do you know all this?

Anil: Dr. Lodha told me so himself.

Vinod: So what are you trying to prove, eh? I

don't know what you are up to, or what Dr. Lodha is up to — but why didn't you bring up all this at the inquest?

Anil: Because it was only this morning that I met Dr. Lodha. Because at the inquest it never occurred to me to look for. . . cracks in the wall.

Vinod: What the hell are you talking about?

Anil: Perhaps a new inquest will bring to light more such cracks? Perhaps it will reveal how a witness was bought over into keeping silent about things she knew? Yes, I'm talking of Tarla Gadgil.

Vinod: You dare suggest that money passed from my hands to —

Anil: Tarla? That wasn't necessary. Just a word in the right quarters and her husband was reinstated in a job from which he had been dismissed because he is a drunken bum. [*Vinod wipes his brow with a handkerchief*] Yes, a new inquest will certainly bring out new flaws, little breaches of the law that were overlooked, little erosions of truth —

Vinod: Since when is it a crime to hold out a helping hand to a starving family? [*still wiping his face*] Let's talk things over, Anil. Let me order you a coffee —

Anil: I don't have the time.

Vinod: [*jeering*] And you have no money! Do you know what the new court proceedings will cost you? I can see you hadn't thought of that. Empty pockets and nothing in your head but a confused notion that —

Anil: [*fiercely*] That brides are not for burning! Not as a ritual sacrifice on the altar of avarice and greed. [*abruptly*] What was the sum for which Laxmi's life was insured?

Vinod: Enough of your foul insinuations! I have nothing to hide. The figure was not large by any standards, a mere eighty thousand rupees policy with the LIC. For tax benefits only, you understand. If you want to check, here is the phone.

Anil: And the policy was assigned to you?

Vinod: [*sharply*] Who else? It wasn't as if she gave me any children. And if by cooking up a few questions you people are angling for some of that money —

Anil: [*standing up*] I find I have nothing more to say to you —

Vinod: Wait!

Anil: [*contempt in his voice*] — because we do not speak the same language.

Vinod: Don't you try your filthy tricks here! I was not born yesterday. Why did you come to me? If you think you can prove that Laxmi's death was not an accident but suicide, you are barking up the wrong tree! Understand? Because she had everything to live for, I can prove it. Yes!

Anil: [*sitting down, slowly*] Did she? I seem to recall a recent amendment of the anti-dowry legislation: if a girl is ill-treated during the first five years of marriage, it will be deemed an attempt to extract dowry.

Vinod: So what are you threatening me with,

you sneaky bastard? Any number of such amendments are passed by different state legislatures every time someone makes a bloody speech or a petition —

Anil: And the sentence is imprisonment for anything from one month to two years; with a fine of —

Vinod: You think you're scaring me? Even if these things are worth the paper they're written on. . . who says my wife was ill-treated in my home? Bring him here to me and I'll call him a liar to his face! Bring Tarla face-to-face with me and you'll see. What did Laxmi lack in my house, I ask you? In the five years we'd been married I took her twice to Kashmir. Bought her a gold watch and a diamond nose-ring. She did all her shopping by car. Can you say your sister did not live well? Have you any idea how much we spend on mangoes every mango season? How lavishly we entertain?

Anil: I'm afraid not. Your hospitality has been a well-kept secret all these years.

Vinod: Non-vegetarian dinners with foreign liquor at 5-star hotels for our business clients — your whole month's salary would not be enough to host one of those. What do you say to that?

Anil: That vulgarity is your modest contribution to society.

Vinod: Air-conditioners, deep freeze, tele ision, video, stereophonic equipment — I have the lot at home. All of it imported stuff.

Anil: What about a vacuum cleaner?

Vinod: What?

Anil: Surely you wouldn't let a vacuum cleaner go without a struggle?

Vinod: [*nastily*] You can have your little jokes, Anil, because you can afford little else! We shall soon be moving into a new flat on Cuffe Parade. The 17th floor of a high-rise building — I bought it last year.

Anil: And this year you bought an eighty thousand insurance policy. [*with quiet emphasis*] Pity you thought of it only nine months before the tragedy.

Vinod: What are you driving at, you brazen upstart?

Anil: [*slowly*] If the fresh investigations prove that Laxmi committed suicide within twelve months from the date of the policy issue, you don't get a paisa on your claim, do you?

Vinod: [*blustering*] So that's your game? Go ahead! Do your worst, you are not even a nail in my sandal! You think I worry about a sum like that? Do you know my annual turnover on the export of grey cloth alone is —

Anil: [*standing up*] I'm not interested. I found out what I came to know.

Vinod: Wait! This is between you and me: when the claim is settled, I'll pass on 10 per cent to you — not one paisa more — on the strict understanding that you make no more trouble. That's eight thousand rupees to keep you sweet, a windfall in adversity — and if you think you can screw me for a bigger rake-off. . .[*shouting hoarsely after Anil as he turns to leave*] Come back! You can have it in cash! All right, you swine, ten thousand! And you can split it any way you like with this Dr. Lodha. . .[*screaming now, as Anil walks off*] Where do you think you are going, you cheap lying shameless dirty crook. . .

[*Pause, while Vinod gets back his breath after Anil's exit; then, in a panic, he taps the phone on his desk.*]

Vinod: [*speaking hoarsely into the phone*] I want a direct line immediately! [*dials a number, waits impatiently*] Mother? Vinod here. We are in trouble, Ma. You know who came to see me just now? Anil!. . . Who Anil? Anil, Anil, Laxmi's brother, for God's sake! He wants to institute a fresh inquiry into Laxmi's death. [*gets up in his agitation*] I'm coming home right away. . . What? Of course I did not lose my head, what do you take me for?. . . I know there is nothing to panic about but. . . [*sitting down again*] All right, then, I'll see you in the evening, but listen, Ma, you can tell Kalu we'll give him the loan he's been pestering us for. . . Yes, all of the two thousand rupees, I tell you Ma — this is no time for bargaining, don't you understand, give him the money and let him go tomorrow. . . No, no, the sooner the better. . . We can cut his salary when he comes back. . . never mind how many years it'll take! And Ma, [*viciously*] get hold of Tarla. . . Tarla, Tarla! The bitch has been shooting off her mouth to Laxmi's sister, otherwise how did they get to know that I had Suresh reinstated in his job? . . .Yes, I'm telling you they do! I could twist her neck! Get hold of her.

[*Blackout*]

Act Two

Scene 3

Tarla's kitchen, the same morning. TARLA *has just finished frying a platter of jelabies and turns off the flame of her stove. She quickly glances at her watch, and is wiping her perspiring face with the end of her sari when there is a knock on the door left, and* MALINI *enters.*

Malini: May I come in, Tarla?

Tarla: Malini! You — you startled me.

Malini: Busy?

Tarla: I've almost finished here — in about ten minutes I'm leaving to pick up my daughter from school. . . Please take that stool.

Malini: [*sitting*] Only for a few minutes, then. I was on my way up to the rogues' gallery.

Tarla: Rogues' gallery?

Malini: Laxmi's in-laws. I thought it was time I paid them a visit. Your kitchen door was unlocked and I smelled something delicious as I passed it.

Tarla: I've just finished frying these jelabies. Neelam loves them. It's her birthday today so I planned a surprise treat. You must taste some.

Malini: I have no appetite this morning.

Tarla: You don't look well at all, your eyes are all swollen. [*pause*] I — I should have come to see you myself. . . to tell you how sorry I was about

— about what happened to Laxmi.

Malini: What did happen, Tarla? You were up there that evening, weren't you?

Tarla: Oh but that. . . [*nervously*] everyone knows what happened. . . Here, let me wrap up some jelabies for you to eat later. [*busies herself with the task*]

Malini: You testified to the police, didn't you? You were one of the witnesses.

Tarla: [*agitated*] I don't want to talk about it any more. I'm not supposed to talk about it any more.

Malini: [*sharply*] Not supposed to?

Tarla: I — I mean it's all finished and done with. My husband will be furious if he finds out I've been talking about it. . . [*attempting a nervous laugh*] You know how I carry on once I get started, my tongue unwinding like a nine-yard sari. . . He was very angry I was mixed up with it in the first place. I only went up there to borrow a cup of sugar, Malini.

Malini: It must have been a harrowing experience for you.

Tarla: Oh it was, it was, I still can't put it out of my mind! I screamed when at last she burst out of the kitchen like a flaming torch — even her long hair was on fire — and collapsed on the floor at our feet.

Malini: [*slowly*] At last she burst out of the kitchen, you said? Does that mean Laxmi was in there long? And you all were waiting for her to come out?

Tarla: I — didn't say that. I only said —

Malini: How long was she inside the kitchen?

Tarla: How should I know? Why do you ask me? I'd just got there with this empty cup in my hand —

Malini: Who was with her in the kitchen?

Tarla: No one, no one, that I will swear! We were outside in the living-room.

Malini: We?

Tarla: Vinod and his mother. Arjun and Kalu. . . Radha had called earlier in the afternoon with her children, but they had already left; and Rani was out. Laxmi had locked herself in alone, of that you can be quite certain, Malini.

Malini: Locked herself in?

Tarla: I mean — she — she —

Malini: Why should she do that?

Tarla: Why ask me? After a row, don't you sometimes lock yourself in a room to be alone —

Malini: So there was a row. What about?

Tarla: It's very late. I must leave now to pick up Neelam. She didn't even want to go to school on her birthday.

Malini: [*sharply*] What was the row about, Tarla?

Tarla: Who can tell? The usual thing, I suppose. . . Laxmi was all dressed to leave with Vinod for a visit to Saher Baba —

Malini: Saher Baba?

Tarla: The holy man whose blessings are sought by women who cannot bear children —

Malini: Go on.

Tarla: And Vinod's mother came out. She — [*whispering and glancing over her shoulder almost*

69

fearfully] she is the kind who would wring the necks of flowers . . . you know that . . . and she began to say things. . .

Malini: What things?

Tarla: The usual things. She said these visits were a waste of time, that Laxmi's womb would remain barren — if it was not already diseased and rotting — because of misdeeds in a past life. . . because one's actions follow one beyond the cremation ground, like a calf follows its mother. . . That only by penance the soul is purified, but she doubted that even if Laxmi fasted to the last grain of rice and drowned herself in the confluence of holy waters at Prayag, the blot on hers could be washed away.

Malini: My God, dear God. . . Go on.

Tarla: And she called Laxmi a cheat because her father had defrauded them. . . And she called her an ingrate because though she had entered their home a pauper, as a daughter-in-law she'd failed in her duty to the family and her husband — set fire to his hopes and his illustrious name and thrown the ashes in his face!

Malini: [*shaken*] God! She said that!

Tarla: That was when Laxmi ran to the kitchen and locked herself in.

Malini: And you all just stood outside the locked door like a captive audience waiting for — what? An accident? Or a command performance by a burning lady?

Tarla: No no, Vinod banged on the door and so did Arjun and Kalu, and I kept calling her name, begging her to open. . .

Malini: Couldn't Vinod have broken open the door?

Tarla: He wanted to! We wanted to but she said — [*stopping fearfully*] Why have you come here, Malini? I've got to go, you've made me late, Neelam hates to be kept waiting.

Malini: Tarla, tell me what she said —

Tarla: I'm late! He'll kill me if he knows I've talked to you! You can't stop me, I'm going —

Malini: All right, go! Just one more thing. Laxmi was very fond of you, you know that, don't you?

Tarla: [*hysterically*] I'm late! So I was also very fond of her! I used to get her to slip down here to wash her hair when they made a fuss about allowing her hot water for her bath. She was kind to my little girl. She was kind to everybody. [*almost crying*] I loved her.

Malini: But at the inquest you only said those things they wanted you to say.

Tarla: Because we must live too, Malini. . . Things have not been so good. There were days with no food in the house when he was without a job. [*imploringly*] We have to live, too!

Malini: [*bitterly*] Of course! You must protect your interests. She was only a friend. Good-bye, Tarla.

Tarla: Your jelabies. . . take them, please. Don't go to see them, Malini, go back home. They might not even let you in.

Malini: Oh but they will! I shall simply ring the bell till the bereaved family opens the door to the surviving sister.

Tarla: Malini. [*pressing the packet of sweets in her hand, then holding her arm*] Don't go up there, don't go! She [*again whispering fearfully*]—she cracks the finger-joints of her right hand and her enemies perish.

[*For answer Malini scornfully pulls free her arm and exits left. Tarla stares after her; then quickly starts to put her sari to rights, runs nervous fingers through her hair, glances at her wristwatch, picks up a cheap plastic handbag and is about to leave when the kitchen door is flung open with a crash to admit the MOTHER-IN-LAW, her greying hair open and flowing down her back, her bare feet and round empty silver tray in hand proclaiming that she has just returned from a visit to the temple.*]

Mother-in-law: So. You've had a visitor!

Tarla: [*petrified*] What — do you want?

Mother-in-law: Who have you been entertaining this morning?

Tarla: No — no one, believe me. I was just —

Mother-in-law: Did I not see her go out of this door with my own eyes? I stood against the wall in the shadows, my bare feet made no sound, she did not observe me, but I saw her! [*advancing on Tarla*] I come from a darshan of Lord Mahavir in the temple, so if you lie to me I shall know! What have you been telling her?

Tarla: I told her nothing — nothing. I was leaving for school — to pick up my daughter. . . Neelam gets scared if I am not on time, so — [*sidling towards the door*]

Mother-in-law: [*blocking her exit*] Where do you think you are going?

Tarla: I told you Neelam gets frightened. . . She throws up if I am late.

Mother-in-law: You are going nowhere. Wretched woman! Snake in the grass! Ingrate! The stench of your deceit had reached my nostrils before I saw that harlot creep out of this door. [*softly*] What did you whisper to her that she will whisper to others?

Tarla: Nothing, nothing!

Mother-in-law: You think you can knife us in the back and get away with it? We put food in your mouths and soon as your bellies are full you think you can defy us? Where is the breadwinner of this house? He will hear of this!

Tarla: [*in terror*] No no!

Mother-in-law: Yes! He was thrown out of work and my son gave it back to him. . . And you! You are just a doll of flesh for him to play with — and you would betray us? [*closing in on Tarla*] What will happen, do you think, when I tell him? When he knows? Will that young head of yours be smashed against the wall like a coconut offered to Sri Ganesh? Or will that soft red lying mouth become bloody pulp at the hands of the butcher you are yoked to for life?

Tarla: [*hands to her face*] No!

Mother-in-law: So now you sweat with fear, do you? What did you tell the sister?

Tarla: [*almost sobbing*] Nothing, nothing!

Mother-in-law: You told her that Vinod got the job back for your worthless husband, did you?

Tarla: No! Never, I swear it on my daughter's head —

Mother-in-law: Why did the sister come to see you? Answer!

Tarla: I don't know, I don't know. . . Please. . . Neelam —

Mother-in-law: — will wait, soiled in her own vomit. How often has that whore come to see you?

Tarla: The first time, the first time, I swear it, since. . . since the accident —

Mother-in-law: What did she want from you?

Tarla: She — she just stopped by on her way up to see you —

Mother-in-law: [*drawing back*] To. . . see. . . me?

Tarla: Yes. She must be there now, in your flat. I must go! Please let me go. It's Neelam's birthday —I —

Mother-in-law: Up there, is she? [*gazing up at the ceiling, cracking the finger-joints of her right hand thoughtfully*]

[*Blackout*]

74

Act Two
Scene 4

A section of the in-laws' living-cum-dining room. On a stool near the dining table the elderly servant KALU is seated, knife in hand, with a platter of french beans balanced on his knees, paring the vegetables lengthwise by holding them between his fingers. At the insistent sound of the door bell Kalu dumps the platter on the stool and shuffles towards the off-stage door, right.

Kalu: [*his walk is arthritic*] Coming, coming. You think I can fly? [*another impatient ring*] You can't let a man walk, eh? [*two more rings as he exits right; the sound of a door off-stage opening and shutting and his voice*] Loud enough to wake the dead!

Malini: [*entering right, packet of jelabies in hand*] I wish I could! Don't you, Kalu?

Kalu   [*following her in*] It's the sister! What do you want? Nobody's home.

Malini: Isn't Vinod seth in?

Kalu: He's at work.

Malini: And Rani?

Kalu: Out.

Malini: Hasn't Radha brought her snivelling brats to visit grandma?

Kalu: Eh? They haven't come today.

Malini: And Arjun? Surely he's stuffing himself in the kitchen. Or perhaps there's no kitchen left — after the fire?

Kalu: Arjun baba is in bed.

Malini: Not ill, I hope?

Kalu: He's on diet.

Malini: Milk and bananas?

Kalu: Just coconut water today. Fruits tomorrow. Vinod seth's orders are that he is not to enter the kitchen or the store-room where they've made place for the new fridge. That's why I've been told to sit here, where I can watch his door. [gesturing towards the open doorway left]

Malini: Poor Arjun. What about baijee? The old lady seldom steps out.

Kalu: She's gone with offerings to the temple.

Malini: To bribe the gods? Good. Then we can have a chat, you and I. [sits on a chair near the stool, leaves the packet of jelabies on the table]

Kalu: I have work to do. No time for idle chatter — they don't like it.

Malini: You were cutting french beans for dinner, I see. Give me the other knife and I'll help you. . . [She resolutely picks up the platter from the stool, puts it between them on the table and begins on the vegetables; Kalu sits on the stool and picks up his own knife] Who does the cooking now?

Kalu: [working] Who does the cooking? Who does anything in this house? Everything went regular as a clock when she was here and now — they expect me to do all the work alone. The cooking. This one won't eat this and that one won't eat that. This one will want her food now, that one an hour later. The washing. The ration. The milk. . . Twice a day I have to stand

76

in the queue for the milk. Then the sweeping, the swabbing. . . am I a god with six hands?

Malini: Of course they must have increased your pay.

Kalu: What's ten rupees more for all the extra work I do? But tomorrow I'm going to my native village. To arrange my daughter's marriage. I told Vinod seth I want two thousand rupees for Sona's wedding. She became a woman three years ago and people are talking. Which father likes to take the sin of an unmarried daughter on his head, eh?

Malini: And Vinod will give you two thousand rupees?

Kalu: [*with a chortle*] He's mean with his money, born with fists so tightly closed, they say it took the midwife a week to open them. Like mother like son, I say. But this time they can't refuse me.

Malini: Why not?

Kalu: Never you mind why not. Vinod seth rang up this morning and tomorrow I'm leaving. By the 9 o'clock train. The ticket even they are buying me.

Malini: They seem to be in a hurry to get rid of you!

Kalu: Eh? She wanted a replacement. But in one day where can I get someone who will do all the work and not steal? Is everyday honest these days?

Malini: No, of course not. An old servant is like a member of the family. Where were you when Laxmi's sari caught fire?

Kalu: Eh?

Malini: Where is the carpet? There used to be a carpet here. I don't see it.

Kalu: It got burnt, they sold it to the rags-and-bottles man. The kitchen table has a new leg, one whole blackened wall had to be repainted. See this burn on my wrist?

Malini: [*inspecting it*] It's a bad one.

Kalu: I got it when we tried to roll her in the carpet. But it was too late. The garland of fire had already embraced her flesh. I fetched the doctor myself. But can a doctor revive a half-cooked corpse with no skin to speak of, eh?

Malini: God! [*the knife slips from her hand*]

Kalu: Arré, you've cut your finger!

Malini: [*shakily*] It's nothing. Only a scratch. Why didn't you break open the door, Kalu?

Kalu: Eh? My shirt was hanging in the kitchen with my month's pay in it — but baijee wouldn't let me break open the door. [*As he speaks, ARJUN, a fat boy in his late teens and a rumpled kurta, is seen lurking in the doorway left*] Even with the smell of burning in our nostrils, she told us to — [*suddenly raising his voice as he sees Arjun*] Arjun baba, go back to bed! What are you doing out of your room?

Arjun: [*coming forward*] You mind your own bloody business.

Kalu: See how he answers? You go back. I have Vinod seth's orders —

Arjun: You can shove them up you know where.

Malini: Hello, Arjun.

Arjun: Oh. What are you doing here?

Malini: Cutting beans. And see, I've brought some jelabies for you.

Kalu: He is not to eat sweets.

Arjun: Suppose you shut up, Kalu, before I push your teeth in?

Malini: Here, have them. [*opening the packet on the table*] They are still hot and crisp. Homemade.

Kalu: Better go back to your room and sip a coconut instead.

Arjun: You want me to smash one on your skull? Thanks, Malini, I'll have just this one. [*helps himself*]

Malini: Do sit. You've lost so much weight since I last saw you, Arjun. If you removed your kurta I bet I could count all your major ribs. You are not fat now. Just healthy. And powerful. Have another. [*he does, seating himself at the table*]

Kalu: When Vinod seth hears you've been guzzling sweets —

Malini: Oh stop it! Arjun is not a child any more and you are not his nursemaid.

Arjun: [*mouth full, and picking up another jelabi*] That's right. Nobody here seems to know I'm not a child any more. . . Next month I start work with Vinod in his office.

Malini: Just don't let them push you around, Arjun.

Kalu: You can push an elephant around?

Arjun: Shut up, bigmouth! [*half rising in his chair*] Just for that I'll give you such a clout —

Malini: Let Kalu be, he's just a wizened old man and no match for you. I bet you could have broken open the kitchen door had you just put your shoulder to it. On the day of the fire.

Arjun: Of course I could have. But Ma said —

Kalu: Never mind what she said. You better get back to your room before she returns —

Arjun: [*roaring*] Shut up! Ma said, "Let her finish what she has started inside there. . ." [*A nervous involuntary gesture of Malini's hand sends the platter of beans crashing to the floor; at the same time, unnoticed by all,* MOTHER-IN-LAW *enters right*] What happened? She's knocked the whole tray of beans to the floor! Don't stand there like an idiot, Kalu. Pick them up!

Mother-in-law: [*authoritatively, coming forward*] Pick them up he will not! And you will go back to your room, Arjun. At once!

Arjun: [*stammering*] M-mother! You're back early.

Mother-in-law: Just in time, I find. What's going on here? Who let her in?

Kalu: She came with some sweets for Arjun baba.

Mother-in-law: Sweep them off the table, Kalu, along with the vegetables on the floor and throw them into the garbage bin. What are you gaping at, you village oaf, be quick about it. Arjun, you should have stayed in your room, those were Vinod's orders. Next time I shall lock you in. Go!

Arjun: I — I won't!

Mother-in-law: What did you say?

Arjun: I'm not a ch-child any more. What — what right has Vinod to bully me, the — the eunuch!

Mother-in-law: [*slapping him*] Such a word you speak in my presence! For my grey hair you have no respect?

Arjun: It's the truth! And don't you ever sl-slap me again, Ma. That's what he is, your Vinod. Eunuch. He should work in a harem. Why did he play the endless farce of dragging Laxmi bhabhi from one holy man to another? Vinod couldn't father a child if you b-bought him ten wives and pushed him into bed with each one in turn.

Mother-in-law: May your tongue fall from its roots for these words against your own brother!

Arjun: He bosses everyone like a gangster! But you think I don't know the doctors have found him without sp-sperm? You think I don't know about the doctors and the tests and all the medicines he's tried — allopathic, ayurvedic, ho-homeopathic—

Mother-in-law: [*screaming*] May your tongue shred into worm-eaten strips in your mouth!

Arjun: — in all forms, all dosages, pastes, powders, p-pills, injections? Perhaps in his next life he'll be born a woman. A nautch girl, with tinkling anklets on her dancing feet!

Mother-in-law: Kalu! Get him out of here and back into his room. You heard? You have overturned a bottle of glue under your feet that you are stuck to the floor? Move!

Arjun: Always Vinod, Vinod, Vinod! [*as Kalu approaches*] I'll break every bone in your body if you touch me, Kalu.

Mother-in-law: Then *I* shall retire to my room. When I come out again, girl, I wish to find you gone. Do not waste your time here looking through keyholes or peering under blinds! And tell your brother not to crane round corners or root in the dirt for a few grubs and maggots. You will only come to more grief, [*cracks the finger-joints of her right hand*] be warned!

Malini: [*standing up*] We are out to discover the truth and to proclaim it! You cannot stop us.

Mother-in-law: It was proclaimed at the inquest yesterday for all to hear. You cannot lay your sister's luckless death at our feet.

Malini: The truth was heard aloud for the first time in this room just now. . . and you may be sure the echoes will resound in the world outside.

Mother-in-law: Take care! We can top all your threats with threats of our own. You people have no claim on us. We make none on you. Is there anything more to be said?

Malini: Yes! You destroyed my sister, you she-devil! And it's better for you that we never meet again. Because if we do, I shall be tempted to kill you!

Mother-in-law: [*smiling*] You think I am afraid of death? When my time comes I shall calmly await it in the holy city of Benares.

Malini: [*hoarsely*] She could have been saved! But you let her die.

Mother-in-law: What is destined will happen. Chaste women have been known to pass through the ordeal by fire unscathed. But can we fight our stars? Our end is ordained before we are born. And we all burn at the end. [*her eyes glow with a strange, fanatic light*]

Malini: You make me sick to my stomach! You murdered my sister as surely as if your hand had sent her up in flames. You are a murderess! [*screaming*] You murdered her! Murdered her!

[*As Malini is screaming "murder", the death of her sister by burning may be enacted, with visual effects, behind a scrim. Blackout*]

Act Two

Scene 5

Same morning, back to the tenement room. FATHER *is standing up, holding the back of his chair for support.* ANIL *is facing him across the room.*

Anil: But where did she go, Dad? She didn't tell you?

Father: She never tells me. She just paints her face. . . and goes. She enjoys it when men's eyes burn holes into her clothes —

Anil: Dad, I must know where she is, it is important. In another few minutes I must rush back to school. I've left my class in charge of a prefect and it must be in an uproar by now. [*as Father turns to shuffle towards the kitchen*] And don't go for your bath yet, wait till Malu returns.

Father: You think I should wait all day for my bath? I am too old for such alien habits. [*pathetically*] Your mother used to have my bath ready at 5 every morning, but what attention does *she* give me? Or the house? [*shuffles towards the kitchen*] She leaves me alone in my cage of bones. . . [*exits*]

Anil: [*calling after him*] Take care, please! You hurt yourself badly the last time you slipped. . . [*enter MALINI by the front door, slowly, like a sleepwalker*] Malu! [*she does not seem to hear him*] Malu! I came back to tell you that you were right about Laxmi's insurance and a whole lot of things. . . Malu, what is it?

Malini: [*a look of sick despair on her face*] Bhaiya. . . it wasn't an accident.

Anil: I know. I saw Vinod in his office this morning. You met the in-laws?

Malini: I called at their home. Laxmi killed herself. They drove her to it, that vicious old woman and her nasty, impotent son. . . [*drawing a deep breath*] What shall we do? [*pause*] You are silent. You think there is nothing we can do?

Anil: [*gently*] Nothing right away, Malu.

Malini: [*violently*] But there is! Stand where you are. Watch me! [*moves towards the trunk*]

Anil: No Malini. I'm afraid there is nothing in that trunk any more. I've removed all the hazards, all the blasts that will now never go off. I dropped your weapons into the bottom of the sea this morning while you slept.

Malini: [*flinging herself at him, beating him on the chest with her fists*] You didn't! They were Roy's weapons! You didn't!

Anil: [*grabbing her wrists*] Stop that.

Malini: He was expecting a raid on his flat and thought they'd be safe with me. What have you done? He is on his way to pick them up. What answer will I give him?

Anil: I shall answer him. He has no right to involve you in his criminal adventures.

Malini: There are crimes and crimes! Cruelties that so far exceed the permissible that to take up arms against them is a duty —

Anil: Guns are never the answer —

Malini: — and degrees of guilt, like the fine markings on a thermometer. . . Feel my head. I'm feverish with guilt, bhaiya. . .

Anil: You are just tired, Malu. Let me fix you a hot cup of tea —

Malini: I am guilty! From childhood there was this fine passion in me for an impossible purity. . . which had nothing to do with being chaste, modest or virtuous — and this I betrayed. Can you understand, Anil, that for the *poor* woman such a self-betrayal is the sure road to whoredom?

Anil: Malu —

Malini: [*a cry of anguish*] Sanjay will never marry me, Anil, though I gave him everything.

Anil: [*going to her*] My little sister, listen to me: you are worth ten of him.

Malini: [*unheeding*] The sexual act may be an occasion of conquest for the man, of surrender for the woman. . . But what I wanted most out of life was to know myself half of a true pair, certain of its integrity. . . This is the only way I know, of overcoming loneliness. . .

Anil: [*quietly*] There are other ways too, Malu.

Malini: But not for me. For me there are only other betrayals, so that if I had a gun just now, I would have turned it on me.

Anil: Only the immediate present belongs to violence. It solves nothing.

Malini: So if the guns solve nothing, we turn to the gods? But for centuries we have taken up battle positions on either side of a great divide

— the haves a mere handful, arrayed in all their strength and splendour against great numberless ragged masses of have-nots — and I know where my place is! [*bleakly*] Repeatedly. . . and most painfully. . . I have been shown where my place is. . . But whose side are the gods on? Is there no Krishna on the field in this Kurukshetra? [*pause*] You have no answer for me, Anil?

Anil: I'm searching for one, Malu. When I find it —

Malini: Don't waste your time. Because I don't really care any more. The final horror, the final betrayal, is that I want to cross over, I want to be where the lights are, where the fun is, where the fortunes are and where it is miserly to count your blessings! Do you despise me? [*softly*] Because a part of me despises myself.

Anil: Don't be a little fool! You think I've never been tempted to. . . cross over? To take up Sanjay's offer and be his henchman for life? To go back to Vinod like a stick-up guy and demand forty thousand rupees as hush money for not initiating a fresh investigation into Laxmi's death, a two-way splitting of ill-gotten gains — yes, he offered me some of the insurance money to "keep me sweet"! . . . You think, Malu, the word "rich" does not have a hypnotic sound for me, too?

Malini: This is great news! My brother is human, after all. And vexed and confused and mortified, like all of us. So what are you going to do? Nothing?

Anil: Nothing till I grow calm inside me first.

You, too, are overwrought, overtired. Lie down a bit, Malu, try to get some sleep. Dad will soon be out of his bath —

Malini: Lie down? Not me! *You* sit here all day like a navel-gazing saint, chanting mantras to Someone who isn't up there [*gazing up mockingly at the ceiling*] to care. I am going. Roy is coming for me and I have to pack.

Anil: What are you saying? I don't understand. You are going with Roy?

Malini: Yes!

Anil: Where?

Malini: Wherever he takes me. [*draws out the battered suitcase from under the bed and begins to collect her articles of clothing from the clothes peg and washline*] I was going to leave a note for you.

Anil: Are you mad? You're running off with a travelling salesman for an improbable revolution? For a Utopia your adult self doesn't even really believe in?

Malini: You don't understand. I have to go. . . to avoid feeling that disgust with myself that I've resolved never to feel again.

Anil: And Roy is going to help you love yourself again? Roy? A man driven by the impetus of hatred?

Malini: I'm not looking for love. If you knew, if you only knew how strongly I feel — after Laxmi's death — the transience, the — the indignity and cowardice of survival. [*a furtive knock on the door*] That's Roy.

Anil: I shall open the door. [*does so to admit Roy, with the large canvas bag slung over the shoulder*] If

88

you've brought that along for the firearms, you're in for a disappointment. They are at the bottom of the sea where I dropped them this morning.

[*Roy takes a threatening step towards Anil, who stands his ground. For a tense moment they take measure of each other*]

Malini: [*hovering anxiously*] I'm sorry, Roy. So sorry this happened. . .

Roy: [*shrugs unexpectedly and turns away*] Don't worry. Those things were ready for the scrapheap, anyway. . . What we really need is the heavy stuff for demolition. . . [*to Malini*] Are you ready?

Anil: She is not going with you.

Malini: Yes I am. You can't stop me, I am needed for this work.

Anil: What work?

Malini: The revolution, which will unite the whole human race.

Anil: [*to Roy*] You think you can achieve a revolution by despatching a few extra people to the burning ghats every day?

Roy: Can you think of a way of making an omelette without breaking eggs?

Anil: Do the jobless men who engage in robberies and derailments and assassinations become revolutionaries or criminals?

Roy: For a keen young history graduate you are a fool. In which subterranean vault do you live? Anything is better than inaction, deadly passivity. . . You have to make a choice.

Anil: If I were called upon to choose between passivity and action which is the result of my creative will, perhaps I would choose action. But you ask me to choose between passivity and a masterplan of operations dictated to me by long-distant thugs who believe not only in sabotage, but random butchery. You ask me to choose the path of death!

Roy: Why not? When the quality of life gets below a certain minimum, we deliberately choose a certain quality of death, in the hope of making life more liveable for others some day. But you choose inertia, stagnation! Yesterday's leavings. . . the warmed up soup, the stale bread. . .

Anil: I choose to be no one's enemy.

Roy: That is just a shallow evasion. Just your bourgeois conscience giving you the jitters! You forget that evil is a part of the human condition. How do you choose to fight it?

Anil: By the way of enlightenment. I am a teacher.

Malini: And teaching offers you such dazzling prospects, doesn't it? I am ready, Roy.

Anil: You can't go. What about Father?

Malini: [turning away] What about him?

Anil: Can you desert him when he most needs you?

Malini: [stung] He never liked me! He never tried to understand the first thing about me! To be born a female according to him is to be born into servitude. All he ever wanted was a son. So I leave him in your care. You will always be there to hold his hand, won't you, Anil?

Anil: He has lost one daughter. He will soon

lose another one — for what do you think your end will be, on the path you've chosen?

Roy: Sure her end will be death, like for all of us. But unlike the vulgar classes, she will come to life at the moment of her death — because it will serve a purpose. Others go out like lights, but she will pass directly from obscurity to immortality.

Anil: You sound like a bad spy movie, you know that? You have to grow up, not to be caught in your own myth-making. You are children who carry things to extremes; adults are more measured, more humble. Think of your father, Malu.

Malini: [*with averted face*] I'm going. [*picks up her suitcase*]

Anil: He is old.

Malini: [*with a shudder*] I don't want to grow old like him. Ever!

Anil: I thought so. You are not really sacrificing your life to make the world a better place, but you think you don't very much want to live. The question then is, are you capable of living?

Roy: What the hell does that mean?

Anil: [*quietly*] That you are only looking for an exit. That to live, you have to love yourself. And to love is to do something far more difficult than to give way to savagery.

Roy: These are the empty generalisations that intellectuals string together to produce scholar-talk! The hot air spouted by sluggish windbags who wish to keep clean of the blood and the sweat and the shit. Let's go, Malini.

Anil: [*to Malini*] You can live with a man who is totally without scruples?

Roy: [*sneering*] You need a minimum per capita income before you can afford scruples.

Anil: [*ignoring him, to Malini*] He has a wife. Your friend, Gita. Has she heard of this arrangement?

Roy: [*loftily*] She knows.

Anil: [*to Roy*] She approves?

Malini: [*quickly*] Of course Gita will be going with us.

Anil: [*to Roy*] Is that true?

Roy: She is going with us as far as Calcutta, where her parents live.

Anil: And where you will ditch her?

Roy: [*with a shrug*] Her Indian attachment to family is the revolutionary's curse. She's never been able to get rid of the bourgeois feeling that she needs a home. But if you form a shell, you have to turn into a snail?

Anil: And my sister, she is different, is that it? You see her leaping like a flea from one temporary abode to another?

Roy: Come on, Malini.

Malini: [*putting down the suitcase*] Answer his question, Roy. I want to know how you see me.

Roy: [*slowly*] I see you as one of those strong flowers with no scent whose roots survive the harshest of conditions — very hard to destroy. In short the stuff militants are made of.

Anil: [*loudly*] You have never been more wrong in all your life!

Roy: [*to Malini*] Are you coming?

Anil: He knows nothing about you, Malu, nothing. However, the decision is yours. I'm off. [*moves to the front door*]

Malini: [*involuntarily stretching out her hand*] Bhaiya. . .! Where are you going?

Anil: Back to school, of course, where my class will be in revolt by now, I'm quite sure. [*stopping short on his way out*] Oh, I forgot to mention it, Malu: Palkar died on his way to hospital this morning. [*exits*]

Malini: [*running forward*] Oh! Anil wait! [*but he does not come back and she stands there stunned*] He's gone.

Roy: [*coming forward*] It's time we did, too. Come on, Malu.

Malini: [*shrinking*] No. I — I want time. I must have time to think. . . Come back for me tomorrow, Roy.

Roy: We're leaving now! [*gripping her arm*]

Malini: I can't. I'm confused. Tomorrow —

Roy: No. Like fire with only that split second in which to kindle or go out. . . you must decide now.

Malini: You are hurting my arm.

Roy: [*applying more pressure*] It is meant to hurt. Why don't you cry out? Why don't you scream? I've never heard you scream, Malini.

Malini: [*unafraid*] What are you trying to do?

Roy: You won't find it so easy to get rid of me, my dear.

Malini: [*with sudden strength wrenching her arm free*] You better go, Roy.

Roy: You fool! What is left for you now if I

leave?

Malini: I've lost out on much, I know, but one road still beckons: I will educate myself all I can. Then there is no future that can be denied me.

Roy: So after all this time you are chickening out on me, you uppity little whore —

Malini: [*with all the force and dignity at her command*] I see now that if I follow you I only exchange one servitude for another. The boot in the face for a place in the kitchen. Brides will not stop burning when you take over the world, Roy. All I can learn from you are new dishonesties, so GO!

[*Like two antagonists they face each other, the suitcase on the floor between them. And in this confrontation it is Malini who appears to gain in stature as the final curtain falls.*]